C.

HOW THE EARTH WAS MADE

WHY PEOPLE SHOULDN'T BE GREEDY

ORCHARD BOOKS
96 Leonard Street, London EC2A 4RH
Orchard Books Australia
14 Mars Road, Lane Cove, NSW 2066
ISBN 186039 702 6 (hardback)
ISBN 1 86039 869 3 (paperback)
First published in Great Britain in **1998**
Text © Margaret Mayo 1995
Illustrations © Tony Ross 1998
The rights of Margaret Mayo to be identified as the author
and Tony Ross as the illustrator of this work have been
asserted by them in accordance with the Copyright, Designs
and Patents Act, 1988.
A CIP catalogue record for this book is available from the
British Library.
Printed in Great Britain

HOW THE EARTH WAS MADE

WHY PEOPLE SHOULDN'T BE GREEDY

RETOLD BY MARGARET MAYO
ILLUSTRATED BY TONY ROSS

ORCHARD BOOKS

HOW THE EARTH
WAS MADE

Before the earth became, there was only
water, and the birds and animals that
swim in it, and the Big Turtle. But, high
above, there was a Sky World where the
Sky People lived.

One day the Sky
Chief's beautiful
daughter was resting
in the shade of a tall
flowering tree when
there was a loud
brr-oomm! and the
tree fell through a
hole in the sky, and
the beautiful girl
tumbled through
the hole after it.

As soon as they
heard the noise, the
birds and the
animals and the Big
Turtle looked up –
and they saw the
tree and the girl
falling from the sky.

"Catch her!" called the Big Turtle. "Someone catch her, or she will drown!"

Then, from every direction, animals came swimming and birds came flying. But it was two white swans who flew up and caught the girl on their strong wings and carried her down.

The swans were anxious. "Big Turtle, what shall we do?" they asked. "The girl is heavy. We cannot carry her for ever."

"Someone must dive down to the deep places and bring up a little mud," said the Big Turtle. "And then I can make an island."

"I'll go!" said the swift-swimming otter. And down he dived.

But the otter's breath was not big enough, and he could not reach the deep places. So he came back with nothing.

"I'll do it!" said the flat-tailed beaver. And down he dived.

But the beaver's breath was not big enough, and he too could not reach the deep places. So he came back with nothing.

The swans were upset. They didn't know what to do. "Help us!" they cried. "Hurry! Hurry! The girl is heavy! We can't carry her much longer!"

Then an old
grandmother toad
said very quietly,
"Let me try. I
might be able to
reach the mud."
And she took a
huge gulp of air,
swelled right up and dived.

Down, down, down she went, and she
reached the deep
places. She filled
her mouth with
mud, and she
began to swim
back. But she
was so tired
that she swam
slower, slower
and still slower.

When at long last she reached the surface, her strength was almost gone. But somehow she managed to spit the mouthful of mud on to the Big Turtle's back.

And the mud spread and grew, spread and grew, until there was an island on top of the big Turtle's back. Then the weary swans carried the girl down, and she stepped ashore.

But the mud still spread and grew, until the whole solid earth was made. And to this day the Big Turtle holds the earth on his back, and whenever he moves, the earth quivers and it quakes.

Now the beautiful Sky Chief's daughter, who fell from the sky, gave birth to twin boys who were not alike in any way. One brother was placid, good-natured and quiet, while the other one was mischievous, noisy and a troublemaker.

Not long after the birth of her sons, the Sky Chief's daughter died. Then, from her body, three precious, life-giving plants sprang up and grew – the corn, the bean and the pumpkin vine.

But the twin boys, they were the ones who made the rest of the world, and, because they were so different from one another, the things they made were also entirely different.

The peace-loving brother was the one who made the rich fertile land, sweet fruits and flowering bushes, the dove and partridge, the buffalo and deer. He made everything that was useful and pleasant.

But the mischievous brother made the
swamps and rough, stony places, the
bitter fruits and thorny bushes, the wolf,
bear, snake and mosquito. He made
everything that caused trouble and pain.

The two brothers didn't agree about anything. They were always quarrelling and so, in the end, they agreed to separate. The peace-loving brother stayed in the east, while the mischievous one travelled westwards, making new things on the way. He made the prickly cacti, the hot dry deserts and the high Rocky Mountains. Those were the sorts of things, he made, and to this day they are still there, in the west.

(A story told by North American Indians) 17

WHY PEOPLE SHOULDN'T BE GREEDY

In distant time, mighty Raven lived in the beautiful Sky Land. He was a bird, big and glossy black, the same as ravens are today. But there was strong magic in his wings and, besides that, he was able to push his beak up to his forehead.

Then he became
Raven-Man, all
cloaked in black
feathers and with
a raven mask on
top of his head.

Once Raven
was doing some
making, and he
made a ball. He
waved his wings
four times, and –
strong magic! it
became the sun in
the sky. Then, for
the first time, it was
light in the world here
below and, because the sun stayed in the
same place and never stopped shining,
there was no night.

Raven looked down and he saw a bare, grey earth plain and empty sea. Nothing more. "What a dull place!" he said. "I must put that right!"

So Raven came flying, but when he landed, he found the earth plain was soft and soggy, like a big mud jelly. He didn't like it. "Here's something else to put right," he said.

He waved his wings four times, and
again – *strong magic!* the mud jelly slowly
dried out and hardened until there were
only a few soft, muddy places left. At the
same time rivers grew, lakes became, and
mountains and hills came rippling
upwards.

"Good!" said Raven when everything
was finished. "Now I must make this dull
place beautiful."

Then he flew
across the land,
swooping and
swerving, circling
and gliding. From
time to time he
waved his wings
four times and –
what then? All
kinds of wonderful
plants sprang up –
moss, fine grasses,
delicate flowers,
bushes hung with
berries, cottonwood
trees, clumps of
birch and forests of
spruce. And, at last,
everywhere was
bright and beautiful.

Now one of the
plants Raven had
made was a wild
pea. In four
days the plant
flowered, and a
pea-pod grew and
grew until it was a
very large,
plump pea-
pod. All of a
sudden, the
very large,
plump pea-pod
burst open
and... *out
jumped a
little man*!

The moment his feet touched the ground, he grew and grew until he was a full-size man. He waved his arms, shook his hands and curled his fingers. He lifted one leg, he lifted the other and walked.

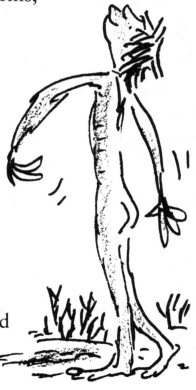

Just then, Raven came flying by. He was surprised when he saw the man. "Who are you?" he asked, "and where did you come from?"

"I came out of the pea-pod," said
the man.

Raven shook his head. "I made that
pea-plant," he said. "But I didn't know
something like you would come out of it.
Still, now you are here, I must teach you
how to live."

So Raven began his teaching. First, he showed the man water and told him to drink it. Next Raven showed him the bushes that had berries that were good to eat, and the man liked the berries so much, especially the raspberries and blueberries, that he smacked his lips loudly when he tasted them.

But Raven was worried. He tipped his head to one side and studied the man.

"You're very big," said Raven. "A few berries won't fill your stomach. I must do some more making."

Then Raven led the man down to a small creek, where there was some clay. With one wing, Raven pushed his beak, like a mask, up to his forehead, and he became Raven-Man. He took some clay and shaped it into two small models of

mountain sheep. He pulled down his beak, became a bird and waved his wings four times over the models, and... *they grew, came to life and bounded away!*

"Oh!" cried the man. He was really excited. "I must catch them!" And he chased after the sheep.

"Come back!" ordered Raven. "I have not finished my making."

So the man came back.

"Listen," said Raven. "You may catch
sheep and kill and eat them. *But don't be
greedy*! Only take what you need."

In the same way Raven shaped more
animals. He always made two at a time,
and when he brought them to life, he
taught the man about them. Raven made the
caribou that is good to eat, and the
muskrat whose sleek fur can make warm
clothes. He made the beaver so the man

could watch and learn how to make a
strong house of wood and mud, and he
made the sharp-eyed mouse, just for
playful fun. He made insects and birds,
some to eat and some just to make the air
lively. Then he filled the rivers with fish
and the sea with fish, seals, whales and
walrus – all things that are good to eat.

As Raven made each pair of creatures, the man became more and more excited, clapping his hands and dancing around. Once again Raven tipped his head to one side and studied him. "I think I must make two more animals," he said.

He became Raven-Man and made two clay models. Then, as Raven the bird, he waved his wings and... up sprang two enormous, growling grizzly bears!

The man trembled. "Ohh!" he gasped. "Ohhh!"

"Good," said Raven. "You are afraid. I wanted you to know what fear is."

It seemed that Raven had finished making. But no. He set to work and made another model. He kept looking at the man as he shaped it, and when he was satisfied he stuck some fine grass on the back of the head and brought it to life and... *there stood a woman!*

"I thought you would be lonely living by yourself," said Raven. "So I have made a woman. Be friends, live together, build a house and have children."

For a little while longer Raven stayed with the man and the woman, and he shared with them some of his secret knowledge. He showed them how to make a fire drill and twirl it until it made a spark of fire that could set a bunch of dry grass alight. He showed them how to make bows and arrows, spears, nets and fish traps. He taught them how to make kayaks that could float lightly on the water, and how to roast meat and fish. He taught them everything they knew.

When Raven had finished his teaching, he said, "Now I must return to my home in the sky, so I ask you both, man and woman, to take care of everything I have made. Don't ever kill or destroy thoughtlessly. Never take more than you need. *Don't be greedy!*"

At last Raven flew back to the beautiful Sky Land. But he did not forget the man and the woman. He often looked down and watched them, and their children, and their children's children...

Time passed, time passed, and Raven married a young Snow Goose, and they had a son, Raven-Boy. And Raven loved his only child with a great love and fussed over him and gave him anything he wanted.

There were now many people living on the earth. Raven looked down. He watched them, and he saw that they had forgotten some of the wisdom he had shared with them. They caught more fish than they needed and left the fish to rot. They were always hunting and killing the caribou, the sheep, the walrus and the seal, carelessly, thoughtlessly, taking much more than they needed. *They were greedy*.

"I must stop them," said Raven, "before they destroy all my creatures." And, there and then, he took the sun out of the sky and hid it in a skin-bag inside his house.

Then it was dark on the earth, and the people were afraid. For them the sun had always been up above, in the same place, brightly shining. They had never known the darkness of night, when only the moon and stars are in the sky.

It was difficult to hunt for food in the dark, so it was not long before everyone was hungry. Then they made prayers to Raven. They laid out their most precious furs and a few choice pieces of food that were left. "Raven," the people said, "Raven, we are hungry. Our children are hungry. We cannot hunt in this darkness. Send back the sun."

After a while Raven was sorry for the people, and he took the sun out of the skin-bag and held it up for short while so that they could do some hunting and fishing. But not too much. Then he hid the sun again, in the skin-bag, and it was dark.

Again the people made prayers to Raven, and again he was sorry for them, and held up the sun for a little while, and then hid it. And so it went on. Sometimes Raven held up the sun, and sometimes he kept it hidden.

Now Raven's son, Raven-Boy, liked to
play with the shining sun, and his father
would let him take it out of the skin-bag
and roll it around inside the house. But
Raven-Boy wanted to take the sun and
play with it outside. He asked and asked.
But this was the one thing
his father would not let
him do, because then
the sun's light could
be seen on earth.

Raven-Boy was used to getting his own way, so – what did he do? One day, when his father was sleeping, he picked up the skin-bag, with the sun inside it, and flew out of the door and up into the sky.

Raven woke, and when he saw his son flying off with the bag he thought Raven-Boy was going to hide the sun and keep it entirely for himself. Raven called out, "Raven-Boy, have pity on the people! Do not keep them always in darkness! Sometimes let them see the sun!"

Then Raven-Boy was sorry that he had disobeyed his father. He opened the bag, took out the sun and put it back in its usual place, up in the sky. He knew his father wanted it sometimes to be dark down on the earth and sometimes light. So then – what did Raven-Boy do? He waved his wings four times, and *strong magic!* the sun began to move across the sky and around the earth.

From that time, on there was order on earth. When the sun rose in the east, day began, and when it sank in the west, night came. The people knew when they could hunt and fish, and when they must sleep and rest. And from that time on, they tried not to kill and destroy carelessly, thoughtlessly. They tried not to take more than they needed. *They tried not to be greedy!*

So, whenever Raven looked down, he was content.

And Raven-Boy – what happened to him? He did not return to his father's house. Instead he chose a wife, and together they flew down to earth, where they lived and had children.

And Raven-Boy and his wife were the great, great, very great grandparents of all the ravens that can be seen today, high in the air, joyfully gliding and circling, tumbling sideways and looping the loop. They have lost their magic powers. Even so, of all birds, the ravens are the wisest. They still have secret knowledge.

(An Eskimo story from Alaska)